READ ALL THESE

NATE THE GREAT

DETECTIVE STORIES

BY MARJORIE WEINMAN SHARMAT

WITH ILLUSTRATIONS BY MARC SIMONT
(*unless otherwise noted*)

Nate the Great
and the
Monster
Mess

by Marjorie Weinman Sharmat

illustrations by Martha Weston
in the style of Marc Simont

Delacorte Press

Published by
Delacorte Press
a division of Random House, Inc.
1540 Broadway
New York, New York 10036

Text copyright © 1999 by Marjorie Weinman Sharmat
Illustrations copyright © 1999 by Martha Weston
The characters of Nate the Great, Sludge, Fang, Annie, Rosamond, the Hexes, and Oliver are based on those originally created by Marc Simont.

The trademark Delacorte Press® is registered in the U.S. Patent and Trademark Office and in other countries.

Library of Congress Cataloging-in-Publication Data
Sharmat, Marjorie Weinman.
    Nate the Great and the Monster Mess / by Marjorie Weinman Sharmat ; illustrations by Martha Weston in the style of Marc Simont.
        p.   cm.
    Summary: Nate and his dog, Sludge, are determined to find the recipe for his mother's monster cookies.
    ISBN 0-385-32114-7
    [1. Lost and found possessions—Fiction.   2. Mystery and detective stories.]   I. Weston, Martha, ill.   II. Title.
PZ7.S5299Natc   1999
[Fic]—dc21   98-39039
                                                                                      CIP
                                                                                      AC

The text of this book is set in 18-point Goudy Old Style.
Manufactured in the United States of America
October 1999
10 9 8 7 6 5 4 3 2 1

For ANNA RICHARDSON WEINMAN,
the world's best mother,
who, by the way,
created the world's best chocolate cookie

—M.W. S.

To my CBI buddies—
Mira, Dwight, Susan, and Ashley

—M.W.

Chapter One
Draculas, Frankensteins, and Werewolves!

My name is Nate the Great.

I am a detective.

My dog, Sludge, is a detective too.

Today Sludge and I had big plans.

To do nothing.

Suddenly I saw something.

There was a note under the door
of my room.

It was written in scribbles.

I knew it was from my mother.

She scribbles when she is in a hurry.

I read it.

Dear Nate the Great,
I lost my RECIPE for
MONSTER COOKIES.
It is on a LONG piece
of paper. I looked
INSIDE the house.
Now I must look OUTSIDE.
When I find the paper
I will be back.
Love,
Your Mother

"I love those monsters,"
I said to Sludge.
"Strawberry Draculas,
Chocolate Frankensteins,
Cinnamon Werewolves.
My mother hates the werewolves,
but she bakes them for me anyway.
I must find that recipe."

I, Nate the Great,
had never solved a case
for my mother.
My mother knew
where everything was.
Until now.
"We will look inside,"
I said. "Perhaps my mother
did not look everywhere in the house."

I, Nate the Great, liked this case.
I could stay home.
I would not have to see
Rosamond or her four cats.
I would not have to see
Annie's dog, Fang.
I could make as many pancakes
as I wanted.

Chapter Two
The Long and Short of It

Sludge and I went to the kitchen.
My mother kept her recipes there.
Each short recipe was written
on one side of a card.
Each long recipe was written
on one side
of a long piece of paper.

The cards were in one pile.
The papers were in another.
My mother liked the cards.
They were all neat and clean.
She did not like the papers.
They were crinkled, wrinkled,
and stained with food.
The pile of papers was a mess.
And it was huge!
But I, Nate the Great,
had to look for Monster Cookies.
"The recipe should be easy
to find," I said to Sludge.
"It's the only one with
drawings of werewolves.
Dozens and dozens of werewolves.
All crossed out.
My mother has never seen
a werewolf she likes."

I spread every sheet on the floor.
I found recipes for foods
I had never eaten
and would never want to eat.
Like Squash Slosh.
I found great names like
Chocolate Bumps and Pecan Plops.
I found scribbled names
that I had never heard of.
Like Lemfan.

There was nothing listed under that one.
And Fig Fizzle.
Nothing was listed under that either.
There were more pages
with scribbled names.
Maybe the recipes
would be added later.
I, Nate the Great,
could not find
Monster Cookies.

Chapter Three
One Big Mess

It was time to think.
I made some pancakes.
I gave Sludge a bone.
We ate and thought.
I knew that my mother
had not made Monster Cookies
for a week.
Today she'd discovered that the
recipe was gone.
So the recipe might have
been missing for a week
or less than a week.

I turned to Sludge.
"We will look in every nook
and cranny of this house.
Look hard. It's for my mother."
Sludge and I looked, sniffed,
climbed up, bent down,
knocked things over,
pulled things out,
pushed things around.

We crumbled stuff.
We jumbled stuff.
Nothing.

"I, Nate the Great, say
there is a big clue
missing in this case.
The clue is my mother.
We have to find her
and ask her questions."

Sludge and I walked toward
the front door.
"Ouch!"
We stumbled over the mess
we had made.

"We will clean this up
when we get back," I said.

Chapter Four
Tasty in Lemon

We went outside.
"Think about where
my mother would go," I said.
Sludge sat down.
"No, don't *sit* and think.
Walk and think," I said.
Suddenly I knew why
Sludge had sat down.
Fang was up ahead with Annie.
I went up to Annie.
"I am looking for my mother,"
I said. "Or her recipe
for Monster Cookies.

Have you seen either one?"

"I saw your mother
three days ago," Annie said.

"She said hello.

Then she looked at Fang.

She kept staring at him.
Then she took a
long piece of paper
out of her pocketbook
and wrote something down.
She said that Fang
would be tasty in lemon.
What did that mean?"
"You wouldn't want to know,"
I said.

Chapter Five
The Best Follow

Sludge and I walked on.
"Maybe my mother is adding
Fang to her list of
tasty monsters," I said.
"I can hardly wait to eat him.
But that does not
help us find my mother."
Sludge turned around.
"Where are you going?" I asked.
Sludge led the way to Oliver's house.
Oliver lives next door.

Oliver is a pest.

Oliver follows people.

Oliver follows animals.

Oliver follows the world.

Oliver was in his yard.

"Oliver," I said.

"Did you follow my mother today?"

"Your mother went out today?"

Oliver said. "Oh, phooey, I missed her!

Your mother is a great follow.
She goes to good places.
Like the fish store."
Oliver collects eels.
He likes anything fishy.
"Oliver," I said, "did you
follow my mother this week?"
"Yes. Three days ago.
It was my favorite follow
of the month."
"Where did she go?"
Oliver looked proud.
He opened a box.
He took out a card.
"I know who I follow
and when I follow them
and where they go," he said.
"I have a card for everybody.
Let's see.

NATE THE GREAT'S MOTHER.
Thursday. 2 P.M.
She spoke to Annie.
She looked at Fang.
She took a long piece of paper
out of her pocketbook.
She scribbled something on it.
It was probably her grocery list.

She went to
the supermarket next.
She looked at the paper.
Then she took a jar
of cinnamon from a shelf.
She stared at the jar.

She put it back.
She bought chocolate,
strawberries, and a lemon."
"A lemon?" I said.

Was she *really* going to make
Lemon Fang Cookies?
"What happened next?" I asked.
"She went to the fish store,"
Oliver said. "She took more long papers
from her pocketbook,
looked at them, and bought
lots of fish."
"Aha!" I said. "More long papers.
They could not be grocery lists.
They must have been recipes.
At the fish store for fish dishes.
At the supermarket
for monster cookies.
What did she do next?"

"I don't know," Oliver said.
"I had to go home
and feed my eels."
"I must go to the fish store," I said.
"I must follow you," Oliver said.
"I know it," I said.

Chapter Six
Something Fishy

Sludge and I walked
to the fish store.
Oliver followed us.
Rosamond and her four cats
were there.
Rosamond was buying tuna.
"Here," she said
to the man behind the counter,
"is some paper to wrap my tuna in.
You wrapped my fish in it
two months ago.
But the other side hasn't been used.
Just turn the paper over
and use the other side."

The paper was stained,
rumpled, and crumpled.
And smelly.
The man made a face.
But he wrapped the tuna
in the paper.
"I recycle everything,"
Rosamond said. "But fish paper
is the best."
I, Nate the Great,
was disgusted to hear that.
I went up to Rosamond.
I did not want to do that.
"Have you seen my mother?
Or her recipe for
Monster Cookies?" I asked.
Rosamond looked mad.
"I saw your mother
a few minutes ago.

She asked me if I
had seen her recipe.
Now *you* are asking me questions.
You always ask me questions.

From now on I will
charge you for my answers."
Rosamond was strange.
Now I, Nate the Great, had
to be even stranger.
"Well, from now on,
I, Nate the Great,
will charge you
for my questions," I said.
Rosamond shrugged.
"Okay, no charge," she said.
"The answer is that I have not
seen your mother's recipe.
And I don't know
where she went
after I saw her."
"For *that* you wanted money?" I said.
Rosamond hugged her tuna package.

"Well, when I answer your questions
I have to think hard,
I have to breathe harder,
my toes tingle,
my cats get hungry,
my . . ."

It was time to leave.
Sludge, Oliver, and I went outside.

33

Oliver took out a card
and scribbled something on it.
Hmmm.
It was just the way my mother
scribbled her short recipes
on *her* cards.

Sludge sniffed the card.
Was he thinking what I was thinking?

Chapter Seven
Crossed-Out Werewolves!

Sludge and I rushed home.
"We have solved the case," I said.
I opened the front door.
We tripped.

"We'll clean up soon,"
I said. "But first we
have to use our clues.
We know that my mother
had the recipe when she
went to the supermarket
three days ago.
She almost bought cinnamon there.
But she didn't.
My mother really *hates*
Cinnamon Werewolves.
So she must have decided
not to bake them anymore.
And that meant she didn't need
all those crossed-out werewolves!
I, Nate the Great, say that without them,
the Monster Cookies recipe
was short enough to write on a card.

So when my mother got home,
she copied the recipe
from the piece of paper
onto a card.
She threw out the paper.
Then she forgot that
the recipe is now on a card."
I went to the pile of cards.
I thumbed through them fast.
I knew I would find
Monster Cookies.
Sludge wagged his tail.
He knew it too.

I looked once.
I looked twice.
I looked three times.
Sludge stopped wagging.
"The recipe is not
on a card," I said.
"I should have known
that my mother *knows*
what she is looking for.
A long piece of paper."
I opened a cupboard.
There was plenty of cinnamon.
My werewolves were safe.
"We have to keep looking
for my mother," I said.

Chapter Eight
The Right Place

Sludge and I rushed to the door.
Thud! Bump! Thump!
We fell down.
"We will clean up
this place soon," I said.
Sludge was tired of hearing that.
We sat there.

"It's hard work being
a detective," I said.

"I have to think about
what I am looking for
and *who* I am working for.
I am working for my mother.
I know that she does not lose things.
She puts things in the right place.
The right place for that recipe
was with the other papers.
She must have put it there three days ago.
So why wasn't it *there*?"
Sludge didn't know.
Neither did I, Nate the Great.
What was important in this case?

Was it important
that my mother had scribbled
something
on a long piece of paper
after she saw Fang?
Was it important
that she bought chocolate,
strawberries, a lemon,
and lots of fish?
Fish could not have anything
to do with Monster Cookies.
Still, there was a clue
at the fish store.
I, Nate the Great,
felt it in my bones.
And up my nose.
It had something to do
with Rosamond's fish paper.

Chapter Nine
A Scribble
Among Scribbles

"Get up!" I said to Sludge.
"We have the clues we need.
Fish paper and lemon."
Sludge and I made our way
back to the kitchen.
I looked at the papers
spread over the floor.

I found the sheet that had
Lemfan scribbled on it.
The paper was stained,
wrinkled, and crinkled.

Just like Rosamond's fish paper.
Because it had already been used
on the other side!
To make cookies.
I turned the paper over.
I, Nate the Great,
read what I knew I would read . . .

Monster Cookies!

There it was.

How to make Strawberry Draculas,

Chocolate Frankensteins,

and Cinnamon Werewolves.

"This case is solved," I said.

"Here is what happened.

My mother had some recipes

with her when she saw Annie and Fang.

She scribbled a note
to buy lemon
on the back of
the Monster Cookies recipe.
Lemfan.
Short for *Lemon Fang* Cookies.
After she shopped and came home,
she put the recipes back on the pile.
But because she had scribbled
on the back of
the Monster Cookies recipe,
it was turned *down*
instead of *up*.
The next couple of days
my mother used other recipes
from the pile.
The pile became very messy.
Today my mother was ready
to make the cookies.

She went to the pile.
She was in a hurry.
She thumbed through
lots of recipes and scribbles.
Like Lemfan.
A scribble among scribbles.
My mother passed it by.
Just the way I did.
If the paper had been blank
we would have known
it was the wrong side.
I, Nate the Great, say that
in this case
nothing would have
been better
than something."
I heard the front door open.
I clutched the Monster Cookies recipe.

I had a big surprise
to show my mother.
I heard a scream.
I was glad that I did not hear
a thud or a bump or a thump.
Sludge looked scared.
I, Nate the Great,
now knew that I
had one more surprise
for my mother
than I wanted.

Sludge and I
were very busy
for the rest of the day.

48pg.